Santa's Snow Kitten

By Sue Stainton

Illustrated by
Anne Mortimer

KATHERINE TEGEN BOOKS
An Imprint of HarperCollinsPublishers

Also by Sue Stainton and Anne Mortimer

Santa's Snow Cat
The Lighthouse Cat
I Love Cats
The Chocolate Cat

Santa's Snow Kitten
Text copyright © 2008 by Sue Stainton
Illustrations copyright © 2008 by Anne Mortimer
Manufactured in China.
All rights reserved. No part of this book may be used or
reproduced in any manner whatsoever without written
permission except in the case of brief quotations embodied
in critical articles and reviews.
For information address HarperCollins Children's Books,
a division of HarperCollins Publishers,
1350 Avenue of the Americas, New York, NY 10019.
www.harpercollinschildrens.com

Library of Congress Cataloging-in-Publication Data
Stainton, Sue.
    Santa's Snow Kitten / by Sue Stainton ; illustrated by Anne Mortimer. — 1st ed.
        p.   cm.
    Summary: Snow Kitten, who lives in Santa's wardrobe, goes exploring on Christmas Eve and ends
up joining Santa on his sleigh as he makes his deliveries.
    ISBN 978-0-06-082714-4 (trade bdg.) — ISBN 978-0-06-082715-1 (lib. bdg.)
    [1. Cats—Fiction. 2. Santa Claus—Fiction. 3. Snow—Fiction. 4. Christmas—Fiction.]
I. Mortimer, Anne, ill. II. Title.
PZ7.S782555Sk 2008   2007021016
    [E]—dc22   CIP
                                                                                        AC

Typography by Jeanne L. Hogle
1 2 3 4 5 6 7 8 9 10
❖
First Edition

To Alex, Sam, and Charlie
—S.S.
For Noah and the best Christmas breakfast, with love
– -λ.M.

IN a wardrobe in a small house in the very north of the world, three kittens were born. Two stripy and shadowy like the night and one purest white.

The wardrobe was full of fur-trimmed red clothes that moved and rippled as the kittens played. On a big brass hook inside the wardrobe door hung a very large sack, a red striped scarf, and a hat with a friendly pom-pom.

BUT best of all, in the corner was a many-pocketed red bag.
The kittens explored each pocket thoroughly.

High up on a shelf, well out of the way, was a big brass
compass, a red picnic box, world maps, tins of travel sweets,
boxes of bells, and even a bright red toothbrush.

Santa's wardrobe was full of everything you would need for a
long, long journey.

FOR the kittens it was a huge place to explore. It was home. When finally they tumbled out of the wardrobe, they discovered a different world. The kittens would follow Santa around, playing and rolling.

But they never strayed too far, and they always went back to the wardrobe to sleep, snuggle, and curl up.

THE white kitten became known as Snow Kitten. The other two were called Shadow and Night, because they blended in anywhere and got away with everything.

THEIR mother was called Snow Cat and she would
tell them all magical stories of the Lemon Moon,
of the North Wind, and of Jack Frost. But only Snow Kitten
listened. His brothers were more interested in causing
mischief and then boasting about their adventures.

Then one day, in the depths of winter, when
the kittens returned to the wardrobe, it was
empty. Where was everything? Where
was Santa?

SNOW Kitten needed to find out, so he left his brothers playing and pouncing.

He had never been downstairs before. It took all his concentration to jump down the steep stairs. But right at the bottom, hung over the wooden rail, was the red striped scarf. Snow Kitten pounced on it playfully.

HIGH on the walls were portraits of the Santa family.
When Snow Kitten looked up at them, they seemed to
look down at him.

Suddenly he saw the red bag propped up by the front door.
Snuggling up against it, he investigated the familiar pockets.
They were all empty.

THEN Snow Kitten gingerly pushed open a door. Warm
aromas of baking, spices, and oranges rushed to greet him.
It all made his nose and whiskers twitch.

He was in the kitchen, and on the chair was the red hat with
the big friendly pom pom.

Snow Kitten scrambled up to greet the familiar hat and could
just about peep over the chair. There on the table was the red
picnic box crammed with a feast of goodies.

Across from it stood a huge iced cake topped with a tiny
figure of Santa and two reindeer. This made his whiskers
very happy indeed.

SNOW Kitten pushed open the next door. Santa's front room was cozy and glowing with firelight, and warming in front of the fire were some colorful stockings.

Pictures of Santa stood on the mantelpiece. Confused, but with nice warm whiskers, Snow Kitten turned around. There on the ironing board were red trousers, pressed and folded.

In the corner, a massive pine tree decorated with reindeer bells jingled at him as he brushed past.

THROUGH another door was Santa's office. There was Santa's desk and his open address book. Pinned all over the wall were maps, letters, and lists.

Over the chair the familiar red coat was slung.

With curious whiskers, Snow Kitten cuddled up against the coat for a moment. Now he knew Santa was nearby.

Then, as he reached the back door of the house, there stood Santa's big black boots, all polished and shiny.

Santa could not be far away.

SO Snow Kitten retraced his steps. But in the office the coat had disappeared and the desk was tidy.

In the front room the ironing board had been put away and the fire was almost out.

And in the kitchen the table had been cleared.

He ran as fast as he could all the way back to the red bag.

But that was gone.

And the front door was open.

Snow Kitten peered out the door.

He sniffed and sneezed as a flurry of snow hit him.

SNOW Kitten ventured out through the open front door into a world where thick snow was draped over everything. It was a world where Jack Frost had breathed glitter and hung diamonds in the trees.

At first Snow Kitten marveled at his sparkling paw prints. He jumped into new powdery snow and pounced on the large, feathery snowflakes that the North Wind gently blew at him.

Snow Kitten had cold whiskers, but he didn't care.

Now he could hide in his own magical white world, and no one could see him.

SUDDENLY the Lemon Moon lit up a trail of sparkly footprints.

Snow Kitten jumped from one to another and followed them all the way to the bottom of a long, snowy field.

And propped by a shed was the red bag.

ONCE again he investigated. Now the pockets were full, one with the red striped scarf and the red hat with the friendly pom-pom, another with the mittens and maps. His whiskers were freezing, so he climbed inside.

He still had to find Santa, but his whiskers were all snuggly and warm. Snow Kitten fell asleep and dreamed of shooting stars and twinkling lights.

SOMETIME later, in another part of the world, a sleigh
stopped on a snowy rooftop.

It was time for a rest.

Santa reached into his bag for his red picnic box and found
a sleepy white kitten.

Santa laughed and laughed. "A snow kitten!"

"Ho-ho-ho!" echoed so loudly around the world that people
stirred in their sleep.

The Lemon Moon smiled, and the North Wind *whooshed*
around happily. Then, from one of Santa's big coat pockets,
there was a friendly noise.

HERE on the snowy roof, Snow Cat greeted her Snow Kitten.

Suddenly Snow Kitten understood the magic of the stories.

The red picnic box was full of a wonderful feast for everyone.

Santa started telling tales of Christmases past. But the reindeer pawed the rooftops restlessly, jingling their bells loudly.

There was still work to do.

With a *whoosh*, Snow Kitten went around the world with Santa and Snow Cat that night.

AT home two shadowy, stripy kittens searched for Snow Kitten all night. They had lots of adventures to tell him about.

But when they finally found him on Christmas morning, curled up fast asleep, it was Snow Kitten who would have the best story of all to tell.